DOWN ON THE RANCH

by
Nancy Fowler Pyle

illustrated by
David Barrow

©2018 Nancy Fowler Pyle (text)
©2018 David Barrow (illustrations)

ISBN# 978-1-7323637-3-1 (hard cover)
ISBN# 978-1-7323637-2-4 (soft cover)

Doodle and Peck Publishing
413 Cedarburg Ct.
Yukon, OK 73099
(405) 354-7422
www.doodleandpeck.com

Library of Congress Cataloging in Progress Number: 2018945706

With love, to my two, dear grandchildren, Josie and Sean.

Nancy Fowler Pyle

To my grandparents, remembering all the happy hours with them going through their daily life, smiling, and sitting around reading the mail.

David Barrow

Grandma and Grandpa
live on the ranch.

1 big, beautiful ranch.

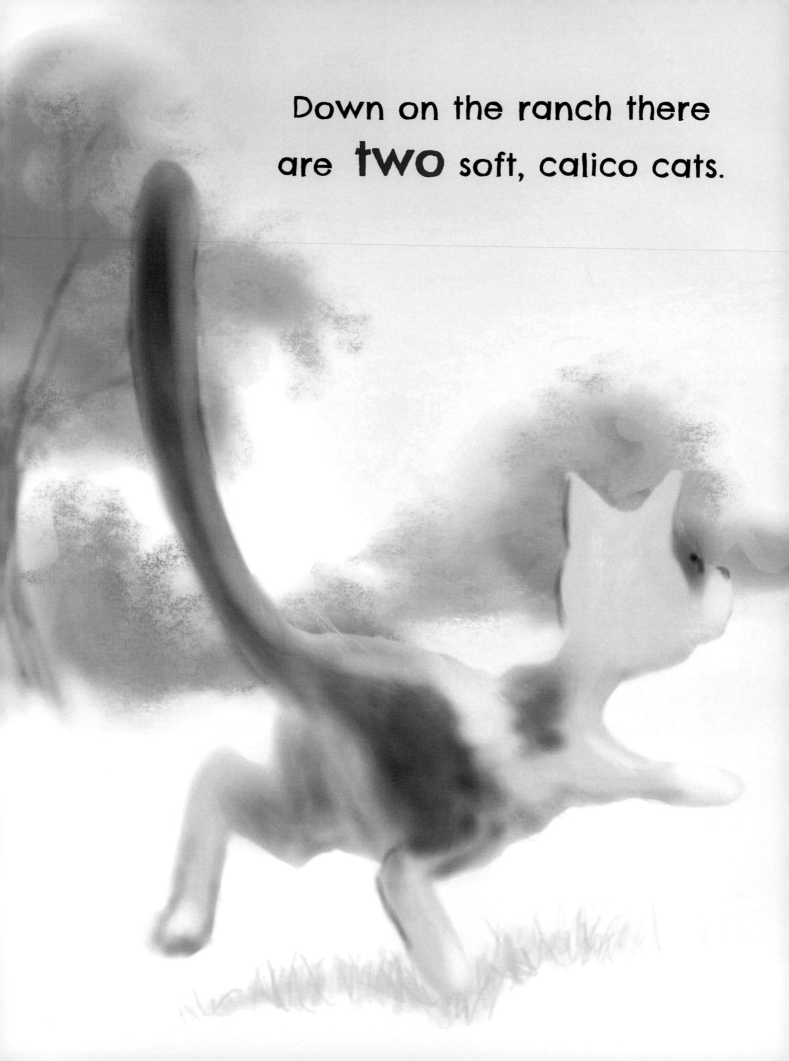

Down on the ranch there
are **two** soft, calico cats.

That's **2** cats on **1** ranch.

Down on the ranch, there are
three trusty tractors.

That's **3** tractors and **2** cats on **1** ranch.

Down on the ranch, there are **four** dependable dogs.

That's **4** dogs, **3** tractors and **2** cats on **1** ranch.

Down on the ranch there are **five** gray geese.

That's **5** geese, **4** dogs, **3** tractors and **2** cats on **1** ranch.

Down on the ranch there are **SIX** pudgy pigs.

That's **6** pigs, **5** geese, **4** dogs, **3** tractors and **2** cats on **1** ranch.

Down on the ranch there are
seven handsome horses.

That's **7** horses, **6** pigs, **5** geese, **4** dogs,
3 tractors and **2** cats on **1** ranch.

Down on the ranch there are **eight** greedy goats.

That's **8** goats, **7** horses, **6** pigs,
5 geese, **4** dogs,
3 tractors, and **2** cats
on **1** ranch.

Down on the ranch there are
nine charming chickens.

That's **9** chickens, **8** goats, **7** horses,
6 pigs, **5** geese, **4** dogs,
3 tractors and **2** cats
on **1** ranch.

Down on the ranch there are
ten coal-black calves.

10 new calves and more every day!
So...

6 pigs, 5 geese, 4 dogs, 3 tractors, and 2 cats...

...all on **1** big, beautiful ranch.

AUTHOR
Nancy Fowler Pyle

Nancy Fowler grew up in Norman, Oklahoma, and attended the University of Oklahoma, where she met her husband, Douglas Pyle. Nancy Fowler Pyle is a retired librarian who lives on a ranch in Pushmataha County, Oklahoma, with her husband of over fifty years, a hundred and eighty cows, and two cats.

ILLUSTRATOR
David Barrow

David Barrow spent his happiest hours in the elementary school library. It was there he read books about famous people and learned how to draw. After working as a graphic designer, camera man, and video editor, Barrow embarked on his lifelong dream of illustrating children's books.

To purchase additional copies of this book or request
an author or illustrator visit, please contact:

Doodle and Peck Publishing
P.O. Box 852105
Yukon, OK 73099
(405) 354-7422
www.doodleandpeck.com

Doodle and Peck

PUBLISHING